Auntie P, Music & Me
All About Animals

Love & laughter!
Pam Atwood

Author: Pamela Krist Atwood

Illustrated by:

About the Author

Pamela Atwood is a gerontologist, dementia specialist, psychotherapist and winner of the bronze National Mature-Media Award 2021 for Total Engagement: Activities for Growth & Expression in Older Adults, co-authored with her husband Thomas (Health Professions Press, 2020). Her current book sprouted from a need and an experience. A friend asked for a book to help pre-teens understand how to relate to their grandmother living with dementia; Pam knew she could help. She thought back to watching her daughter, Charlotte, and Pam's cousin, Pat who had young-onset Alzheimer's. She hopes it helps your family too.

Although Auntie P, Music & Me is about animals and music, there are also tips Pam provides to her caregiver coaching clients. See if you can find in this book:
- The benefits of tapping into long-term memory
- The use of reminiscence
- Asking "tell me about it"
- Recognizing good days and hard days
- Differentiating between giving someone a hard time and having a hard time.

For more information on dementia or to learn how to be a confident caregiver, visit AtwoodDementiaGroup.com. Finally, a portion of the proceeds of this book are being donated to CaringKind NYC and the Alzheimer's Association-CT Chapter. If you need help 24/7 you can reach out to Helpline@caringkindnyc.org or call 800-272-3900.

I love my Auntie P.

Her name is Pat and her nickname is "Party On Pat."

She has a problem with her memory, but her love for me and for the things that make her happy is still the same as always.

Sometimes Auntie P says thing that confuse us. My mom calls them "her hard days" because she's having a hard time.

Auntie P really loves music. And I really love animals.

This is a story about how much I love animals and how much Auntie P loves music. This story is also about how we figure things out, so they aren't confusing anymore, and how I help my Auntie P.

Last week we went to visit Auntie P. She was listening to music, but it wasn't the music that makes her happy. I don't like to see Auntie P unhappy – that's not who "Party On Pat" is. I told her about a new song we are singing at school. Then I asked, "Auntie P, what music makes you happy?"

"Oh, I really love the Beatles." This was confusing. How could beetles make music? I thought maybe her memory was having a hard day. I said, "Tell me about it."

Auntie P smiled and looked out the window as she said,
"The Beatles were my favorite band." They were also
called the 'Fab Four' and were popular all over the world.
One of my favorite songs was "Here Comes the Sun."
I also love "Yesterday" and "Hey Jude"
"Twist & Shout" and "Let it Be".
They had so many wonderful songs.

Auntie P had a big smile on her face now. I asked her about some other music she liked."I used to sit on the floor of my bedroom and listen to the Monkees," said Auntie P.This was confusing. How would monkeys make music? I thought maybe her memory was having a hard day. I said, "Tell me about it."

Auntie P smiled and put me on her lap. "The Monkees were fun to listen to, and they had their own TV show. I loved singing along to "Daydream Believer."

I never knew Auntie P liked music so much. I asked Auntie P if she listened to music every day and she said, "Yes. Some of my favorite music was by The Eagles."I know that eagles make noises when they fly, but music? This was confusing. How would eagles make music? I thought maybe her memory was having a hard day. I said, "Tell me about it."

Auntie P smiled and hugged me. "The Eagles were very popular in the 1970s. My favorite song was 'Take it Easy', but they had many hits."

"I didn't know birds made music," I said giggling.
Auntie P gave me a high five and said,
"Let me tell you about the others…"
"There's the Flamingos…"

"My dad, your Grandpa Eddie, used to listen to them. And when he put on their album, he and Grandma Elaine used to dance in the kitchen. Their favorite song was 'I Only Have Eyes for You'."

Auntie P also told me about the Penguins…

She said, "The Penguins sang "Earth Angel" and it was played at all our school dances."

Auntie P then took me by the hand and started singing a song while we turned in a circle. "There was "The Byrds" who sang 'Turn! Turn! Turn!' That one really made me think." And she sang, "…there is a season…turn, turn, turn... And a time to every purpose under heaven…."

We laughed and sat back down. I thought maybe today wasn't a hard day for her memory. I wondered if there were other songs that made her happy, or made her think, or made her sad.

"The Turtles sang one of my favorite songs and we can sing it and be happy together!"

"Imagine me and you…. I can't see me loving no body but you… So happy together…"

I asked Auntie P if she could think of the happiest song she ever heard. She thought and thought. "You know sweetie, sometimes my memory doesn't work well. But when it comes to music, I feel like I can remember and feel, and be myself. Music is a very special gift. It makes me feel joyful…OH. I know," she said, "Three Dog Night!" This seemed confusing, but I said, "Tell me more Auntie P!"

JOY TO THE WORLD

"They sang to their audiences that "ONE is the Loneliest" and then told us about a bullfrog named Jeremiah! He was a good friend – JOY TO THE WORLD"

Auntie P has a memory problem. But she remembers a lot when she thinks about music. And when I ask her about it, she sings, and dances and we know we love each other. Even with a memory problem, we can be happy together.

Suggested playlist for this story:

- Here Comes the Sun, Yesterday, Let It Be and Twist & Shout ~ the Beatles
- Daydream Believer ~The Monkees
- Take it Easy ~The Eagles
- I Only Have Eyes for You ~ The Flamingos
- Earth Angel ~The Penguins
- Turn! Turn! Turn! ~The Byrds
- So Happy Together ~The Turtles
- Joy to the World ~Three Dog Night

The End